Mended with Gold and epilogue Out Loud

By Lee Welch

Character, like a photograph, develops in darkness

– Yousuf Karsh, photographer (1908 – 2002)

Trademark Acknowledgments:

Canon

Skype

Wal-Mart

Honda

Dr Martens

Terminator

Google

Superman

Batman

Mickey Mouse

Instagram

Uber

Tiger Balm

ISBN: 978-1-0670221-0-5

www.leewelchwriter.com

Chapter One

The first house Alex looked at had black mould creeping up the bedroom walls. Next was a place with a pump in the cellar because 'the creek floods in a storm, but it's nothing to worry about, mate'. Then came a house with a sunlit patio, glaring white, with palm trees in pots. Something about the light and dusty foliage reminded him of Laos and he backed out speechlessly, eventually managing a curt 'no thanks' to the bewildered agent.

Next was an apartment, outside which a dog barked as tirelessly as a metronome, then a house that smelled of rot. Followed by a 1920s villa next to the local landfill.

And then came a house with a handsome young man asleep on an old Chesterfield in the sunroom.

Alex paused in the open doorway, briars from the overgrown garden catching in his hair, the roar of sea and wind loud in his ears. A lot of old houses in New Zealand had these sunrooms. They were like glassed-in verandas; bright, warm places. They didn't usually contain a sleeping beauty.

The sleeper was in his twenties, thin, with tangled dark-brown hair and pale skin. He was gorgeous in an angular, surprising way, with long eyelashes and a wide mouth. He breathed quietly, at peace, cheek pillowed on one hand, giving Alex the intimate sort of view he'd get if they woke up together in the morning.

If Alex was bloody lucky, that was.

Sleeping beauty wore a too-big sweater patterned with green and beige snowflakes. He was young enough, and handsome enough, that he was probably wearing it ironically. Some of Alex's students dressed that way; deliberately dowdy, deliberately geeky, knowing it only made them cuter. Alex's eyes scanned down. Took in faded black pants that were spattered with—blood?

Alex took a step backwards, heart beating faster, before taking in other colours—pale blue, canary yellow—and realising that blood wouldn't show up on black anyway. It was paint. So, a house painter? An artist? If the latter, he probably thought photography was only for selfies and not really art. His feet were bare, but by now Alex knew that didn't necessarily mean he was a vagrant, as it would have in London, New York, or Toronto. Shoes were often optional in New Zealand, and in a beach settlement like this one, they were probably more optional than ever.

There was something about this sleeper, though, that suggested poverty. His bony wrists spoke of meagre dinners, and the soft skin under his eyes had the bruised look of the terminally exhausted. Alex recognised it all too well from the mirror.

Nonetheless, it would have made a fine photograph; the sleeping man, lips parted, vulnerable, a shaft of afternoon sun hovering above him like a visiting god. There was something at once mythic and commonplace about him. He was a modern Endymion, down on his luck, ugly Christmas snowflake sweater and all. Ideally, he'd be naked. The flowery upholstery of the Chesterfield had faded to soft greys, like tumbled clouds. A disintegrating paper lantern hung from the ceiling. The lighting would be tricky, with the sun like that and the subject in shadow.

Alex had a camera; his favourite old Canon, with a standard lens. He'd been planning on taking pictures of the house. He itched to take a shot now, but for portraits of people he always asked, and to ask would be to wake the sleeper and ruin the shot. This was one of those moments you let go by then remembered ever after at three in the morning. At least, this would be a beautiful image to conjure with in the small cold hours.

But who *was* this young man? Had he broken in to steal something and, finding the place empty, decided to take a nap? *Was* he a vagrant? According to the estate agent, the house had been empty for months. The door to the sunroom hadn't been jimmied, and although one of the windows at the far end was cracked where the bushes outside had grown too close, there was no obvious break-in.

In a way, it was none of Alex's business. It wasn't his house. Though the moment he'd seen it, nestled on the hillside, half hidden by long grass and overgrown shrubs, he'd felt the same internal jolt as when he'd come across sleeping beauty— something inside him saying, *yes, oh, yes.*

The house was small, old, and weathered. It had once been painted blue, and was now a speckled grey. 'Not flash' the locals would say, but its box-like, 1950s simplicity was appealing, unpretentious. It hunkered down in the wind, gazing north through a row of identically sized rectangular windows. Getting out of his car, the roar of the wild west coast had filled Alex's ears, the sky misty with salt spray. He'd waited a minute or two for the estate agent, then felt like taking pictures of the house, and found his way to the sunroom.

On the dusty floorboards, next to the Chesterfield, lay a dog-eared paperback. An intruder who broke in to read? Alex took in the front cover and gave a huff of disbelieving laughter, for it was *The Thief's Journal,* by Jean Genet. He put a hand over his grin, as if the young man might see it and think he was being laughed at. But it was so unexpected, so perfect, that it was difficult to stop smiling.

So, this sleeping beauty liked literature. Gay literature, too.

What colour would his eyes be? He looked European. His eyes could be blue, brown. Green would be stunning.

From far away, just audible over the rush of wind and sea, came the drone of a car engine. Alex pulled out his phone. Four twenty. That would be the estate agent with the keys. Finally. He glanced again at the sleeping face, the tumbled hair. Should Alex wake him? Tell him to go? Stop him getting into trouble?

But something made him turn away. Perhaps it was just bone-weary reluctance to talk to anyone he didn't have to, even an attractive young man. Perhaps it was a kinder impulse, because there was something about those thin wrists, tatty sweater, and tired face that made him feel that here was a person who would rather not be found.

Alex picked his way back to the road through the brambles and bleached grass, and slammed his car door several times, as loudly as he could. On the final slam, the agent drew up, apologising, tugging his tie and smoothing his hair uselessly in the wind. Out here, against the wild hillsides and the flax bushes, the agent's blue business suit seemed a bit ridiculous. Alex smiled, shook hands, made all the usual noises. His thoughts kept returning to the sunroom, warm and golden. Sleeping beauty couldn't be a thief. In this house, there was nothing to steal.

The agent opened the front door and Alex went in to the echoing living area. There was an internal door to the sunroom to the right. The internal door was glass, covered by a faded red-and-white gingham curtain. It was impossible to see whether the sleeper was still there or not, but Alex thought he heard a creak and the quiet scuff of bare feet.

He turned his back to the sunroom door. The living room was long and narrow, north facing, bright, stale from being shut up. Bare boards, not polished. The walls were a dirty grey-pink, the windowsills scurfy with peeling paint. Of course, there was no radiator; all New Zealand houses were cold and miserable in winter. At least, there was a squat wood burner in this one, its thick glass door cloudy from years of flame and smoke. To the back of the living area was an open-plan kitchen, with a stainless-steel sink, and cracked brown linoleum. Three empty jam jars stood on the countertop, gathering dust.

Everything was dusty, and yet, the room had charm. It was warm and light. It felt safe and private, a place he could relax. The view was dramatic, with the bowl of the valley and the road disappearing between towering hills to the north. There were only four other houses to be seen, all shabby, all facing the sea, which was only a few hundred metres away. If he stood at the windows and looked left he could see the pebbled beach, and the turquoise chaos that was Kahawai Bay, the surf breaking white on black rocks. What would it be like to be here in a winter storm, with a fire blazing in the old burner?

He inspected the rest of the house—two bedrooms, both tiny, one at the front and one at the back. Both rooms would take a double bed, but not much else. He could, of course, get a single bed, but that idea was so sad he closed the bedroom door and went into the small washroom. To shower, he'd have to climb into the old claw-footed tub and use a rusty shower hose that was set way too low. There was a Victorian-looking toilet with a chain pull. An empty airing cupboard. A tiny laundry area by a warped back door. The door opened out onto a small flat area choked with weeds, amongst which stood a modern plastic water tank and a disintegrating woodshed.

By the time they got to the sunroom, it was empty except for the ancient Chesterfield. The agent stood beneath the paper lantern, into which insects had eaten a delicate filigree, and talked about internet options. Alex nodded, not listening. He wanted to get that old lantern, put a light in it, see how the shadows fell. The room had already lost the sun, because shiny-leaved shrubs had grown up outside. He'd cut them back hard, when the place was his.

If. *If* it became his.

Because it would be stupid to take it. In traffic, it would be a forty-minute drive to the studio in Wellington. The closest shop was fifteen minutes away down a road like a switchback. He shouldn't buy a house because a trespasser with good bone structure and a taste for Genet had happened to fall asleep in it.

No, but he might buy it because it felt like a harbour in a storm. The wind buffeted the place again. The house creaked, in a way that was already familiar. He didn't want to leave.

The agent locked up and they stood on the cracked concrete step at the front, looking out over the flax and brambles and the restless sea. The light had turned red, drenching the rugged hills in kirsch.

"So, about the internet," Alex said.

The agent was battling with his tie, which kept flapping in his face. "It's dial-up or a satellite service, like the farmers use. No fibre, out here."

"Mobile reception's patchy, eh?"

"It's the hills, I'm afraid. It's all right at Makara Beach. That's the next bay along, where the settlement is. Or you could go up top." The agent waved a hand at the closest hill, which was nearly perpendicular. "What do you do, Mr. Cox, if you don't mind me asking?"

"I'm a photographer." *Or I was. These days I'm more of a fraud.* "I teach a photography course at the local Tech, too. I'd need that satellite internet." *Yeah, because the stock libraries can't wait to get my next picture of a dandelion clock blowing in the wind.*

The agent nodded, gaze on the glowing hills. "It's a lifestyle choice, this place. I have to tell you, the road closes sometimes. There are slips. Whole settlement gets cut off. It can feel very isolated in the winter. Very wild in a storm. Takes a particular kind of person to want all that." His voice was taking on a resigned tone. Alex could see him thinking 'no sale'. "Lovely spot though, isn't it, on a day like this?"

That evening, Alex sat in his neat rented apartment in town and ate chili prawns with snow peas. They'd taste better if he'd spent the day sanding windowsills in the sea air. He rang his folks in Toronto and told them about the place. Mom said it sounded beautiful and he should do whatever made him happy. She asked about his work, about New Zealand winters, and when he might visit Canada again, and all the time her tone was pleading, 'Tell me you're all right, tell me you're content, tell me you're better.' Dad asked about drains, piles, and water supply, then told him to go with his gut.

He Skyped his old colleague Marilyn in London. Once, he'd called her a friend. These days he never knew what to talk about, but he owed her several calls, and finally he had something to say.

Her eyes were bloodshot, with black smears where she hadn't taken off last night's makeup. Her hair—currently blonde at the roots and black at the tips—was all anyhow. She wore a silky robe, bright with Japanese-style cherry blossoms.

He told her about the house.

"It's a midlife crisis," she said. "Seriously, don't buy a house in Tinpot, New Zealand. You'll regret it. Get a convertible instead."

"I want the house."

"Geez, and I thought Wellington City was the ass-end of nowhere. Could you get any more remote than this beach place?" She yawned. "It sounds worse than Saskatoon."

"That's why I love it."

"What does whatshisname think?"

"That's over. What's that got to do with it anyway? This house is for me."

"You'll meet someone eventually and he isn't going to want to live in a tin shack with hillbillies shooting each other over the—" She glanced away. "Well, you know what I mean. You realise it's eight o'clock in the morning here. *Saturday* morning." She yawned again, hugely.

"There aren't any hillbillies. It's mostly civil servants and old hippies as far as I can tell. It's a civilized backwoods. Big night, last night?"

If he'd still been in London, he'd have been out with her. Would probably now be nursing a hangover of his own. Except, these days, he didn't drink. Because last time he'd left a bar he'd ended up cornering a jaywalker who'd nearly stepped out in front of a bus, yelling until the youth was crying and someone called the police.

Marilyn shrugged, waggled her head to indicate 'yeah, sorta big', and winced. "What if you spend all your money doing this place up then hate it and can't sell it?"

"I won't hate it. I wish I was there right now."

"Are you sure you're not running away? Geez, darling, are you sure this isn't all part of the post-traumatic stress?"

"I'm fine." *Though I may have lied slightly to the psychologist.* "I'm just old and tired. I'm forty-five. Don't you get sick of the divas and the dawn starts and the shitty hotel rooms? I want a more regular life. I like it out there."

"You're at the peak of your career and you're shooting suburban weddings and corporate away days. Listen, if you won't buy a convertible, for God's sake, take a younger lover. You know you have that Jeffrey Dean Morgan thing going on. They used to fall all over you. Pick someone sweet who'll worship you. It'd be more fun than saddling yourself with a log cabin in Hicksville."

"Someone who'll *what*? You know how *awful* that sounds? I'm buying the house. It's pure, out there. Clean. The light's amazing and the locals wear gumboots to the shops. They wear those Christmas snowflake sweaters in April. No one cares."

Sleeping beauty had popped into his mind again. Why did that feel like a good omen? He didn't believe in omens. If he told Marilyn, she'd really think he'd lost it.

"It's people of Wal-Mart, Alex. It's a slippery slope. Next, you'll be buying a onesie. You'll never have sex again. You buy this house, you're doomed."

Next morning, he made an offer.

* * *

It wasn't idyllic. When a northerly blew, the house could have been at sea. The rain roared on the tin roof and the windows bowed and shivered. The first windy night, he sat up until nearly dawn, expecting at any minute to be picking broken glass out of his bed. Cold draughts came up from between the floorboards, and it was always five a.m. when he discovered he was out of coffee and milk. He couldn't find the key to the woodshed behind the water tank.

But nothing reminded him of Laos. Nobody bothered him. And the photography studio where he sometimes picked up work seemed to accept that he couldn't appear at a moment's notice any more. He went running in the hills, spent a lot of time just sitting, watching the sea and the birds and the wind-whipped grasses. He changed the locks, just in case, and found that in the afternoons it was impossible to stay awake on that faded old Chesterfield in the sunroom. Peace crept closer.

Best of all, he felt like taking photos again. He *wanted* to.

On a rare, still day he went down to Makara Beach and spotted a tern diving repeatedly, a white arrow into a swirling bed of kelp. Nearby, also in the water, a woman in a black wetsuit collected something, maybe crayfish, maybe the abalone the locals called paua. He set up his camera and tripod. If he timed it right, he'd get a shot of the silver diving bird and the glistening black woman, both inhabiting the same space for an instant.

He saw, out of the corner of his eye, that someone was collecting firewood on the beach behind him, but the guy kept his distance, dark hair blowing across his averted face. He wouldn't be coming over to make comments or ask questions. Alex could always tell.

So, Alex didn't notice, until the guy was well past him, that around his waist, partially hidden by an old grey coat, was tied a hideous sweater with green and beige snowflakes. Alex froze over his tripod, shot forgotten.

Sleeping beauty was carrying his driftwood bundled in a ripped piece of tarpaulin. He cradled it against his chest in an odd defensive attitude, as if expecting thieves to dart up and snatch it away. He walked without grace, hunched like an awkward teenager, stumbling over rocks. He got to the place where people parked their cars, put his wood into the boot of a shitty-looking white Honda with one red door, got in, and drove away.

Alex turned back to his shot, but the woman had come to shore and the moment had passed. Everything felt flat and grey. Sleeping beauty's spell had been broken. He was a gawky local with no dress sense. He probably used paperbacks as kindling and his girlfriend threw him out when he drank too much. The memory of him asleep in the sunroom warred briefly with reality. Funny how the way a guy moved and held himself could be such a turn-off. The tern was still diving further out, but the light had gone. Never mind. Alex lived here now. Plenty of chances to get that shot another day.

He was starting to meet the locals. The people who ran the café in Makara Beach. The old guy in the towelling sunhat, who checked Alex's water tank and pronounced it sound. Frank, who lived on the estuary and was fond of herons and native grasses. Matire and her kids, who offered Alex a taste of a raw sea urchin—*kina* they called it—on the beach, and laughed at the expression on his face when he tried the salty, gritty, slimy stuff.

Juleke was Dutch and ran a tiny art gallery from a converted garage in Makara Beach. He met her out fishing one day. She had a bucketful of stinking bait, masses of greying blonde hair tied back with a rubber band, and a pleasant, if talkative, manner. She also ran a local art group once a month, and Alex found himself being roped in to giving a talk about photography.

"We love guest speakers. Any sort of art. We had a quilter once; I think that's an art, don't you? We've never had a photographer before. There's a lot of talent around here, you know. We meet at Edith's house. That's the grey one on the corner in Makara Beach. You know it? Well, Edith used to be a big set designer on Broadway. And you'll meet Linda and Margaret." She was ticking people off on her fingers, fishing rod wedged into the rocks. "And Albert. And Beryl, who has the place with the paua shell fence. And Joe, who keeps the gallery in business." She had a lot of laugh lines and they all crinkled. "No one buys my stuff much. You must come to the gallery next time you're passing. Maybe you'll see something you like? Anyway, it's great you'll give us a talk. Thursday at six. At Edith's. Makara Beach. You know where to come."

He walked away with a sinking heart, wishing he'd said no. But these people were his neighbours and this was a small place. Kahawai Bay had only six houses, Makara Beach about thirty. Best to be agreeable about the art group. Especially since he had no intention of going into the gallery. He knew what he'd find: over-bright acrylics and tentative water colours. Earnest sunsets. Fussy painted beach pebbles that would have been nicer left alone. He'd have to look around, pretend to like stuff, profess lack of funds and buy a postcard before he could leave. The idea exhausted him. He was reverting. Turning back into the teenager with acne who hid behind a camera at gigs because he was too shy to talk to people. And what good is a professional photographer who can't put people at ease?

He went home, locked the door, and lay on the old Chesterfield. He wondered if sleeping beauty's name was Albert, and if his paint-spattered pants meant he frequented art groups with middle-aged ladies. Then he laughed at himself and, glancing up, noticed the insect-nibbled paper lantern. He fetched a light and a camera and the afternoon became about shutter speeds and angles, and that night he slept, all night, for the first time in a long time.

* * *

Edith's house was big and square and storm-scoured grey. The blinds were always drawn. Approaching it on Thursday evening felt like walking towards the creepy house he'd passed every day on his way to elementary school. But inside it was all cups of tea and old ladies and a convivial hum of conversation. It was like being at Grandma's house. Nothing mattered. There was no one to impress. It felt like a larger version of his own place at Kahawai Bay. He was the youngest person in the room by a decade.

Edith was tiny, with enormous Iris Apfel glasses and bright red lipstick. Her accent was resolutely Kiwi, except for the occasional surprise vowel, which she flattened like a New York native. There was a semi-circle of chairs, most of them occupied, and a coffee table for his laptop. He accepted a cup of tea, and chatted to Edith about New York in the seventies. On the wall was an enormous Warhol; bright, simple flowers. Edith had met Warhol several times. And Diane Arbus, too.

Then a young man came in clutching a sketchbook, and Edith could have been speaking in tongues for all Alex understood her next few remarks. Because it was sleeping beauty. Except, awake, he wasn't a beauty at all. He could have been, but he hunched like a teenager trying to hide new height. His hair straggled in his eyes and curtained his cheeks. He looked mostly at the floor. He'd ditched the green snowflake sweater and wore a plain black one, black jeans, and a pair of ancient Dr. Martens boots. But he wore it all with zero style. The green snowflakes were clearly no ironic gesture; he probably just wore the thing because it was warm.

He made for the kitchen with the air of a regular visitor, got a mug of tea, then hovered in the doorway uncertainly, sipping tea, sketchbook still pressed to his heart. He glanced at Alex. His eyes were brown, with dark smudges beneath them as if he still hadn't had a good night's sleep. Then he caught Edith's eye and smiled, and was gorgeous again. *Damn.*

"There's Joe," Edith said. "We can get started."

Joe. It seemed an old-fashioned nickname for a guy in his twenties. As if aware of being considered, Joe glanced at Alex again and ducked his head, blushing. Interesting. Kind of cute. If only he would stand up straight and show that handsome face to the world. Was he shy? Or did he know Alex was the new owner of the house in Kahawai Bay? Perhaps he felt guilty for trespassing?

Joe sat in a chair a bit behind the others and curled over his tea, now appearing sulky. Perhaps he was annoyed at having been banished from the warm sunroom. Alex had once liked sulky boys. They were more of a challenge, and he felt a deeper sense of triumph when he made them whimper and wriggle like puppies. What on earth was Joe doing here, like a crow in a flock of partridges? Fulfilling a social obligation? Yet, he was far too old to be made to go somewhere with Grandma, so he must be here by choice. For art. The uncared-for hair gave him a hippy-ish vibe. Maybe he painted mandalas? But it could just as easily be pictures of cars with flaming wheels, or fantasy sunsets with dragons and women in metal bikinis.

Juleke called for quiet and introduced Alex to the group. She'd done her homework, read out a bit from his website, mentioned the awards he'd won. His stomach gave a sick lurch. Was she going to mention Laos? Why had he not thought ahead? Should have asked her not to.

But she didn't. Either her search hadn't thrown that up, or she had some tact. All the same, when he opened his laptop, his hands were shaking.

He'd selected three photographs to discuss: a Cartier-Bresson, an Arbus, and one of his own—a shot of dancers from the New York ballet, hanging about backstage, bored and beautiful, sharing a bag of corn chips. After the photo discussion, he added a bit about the use of photography by painters, figuring that would be relevant. That took him up to twenty minutes. He hadn't been sure how to pitch it, but it went down fine. Except with Joe, who seemed to be struggling to stay awake.

Alex felt the same spike of irritation as he did when students texted in class. Usually, he'd say something pointed, or ask a question to see if they'd been listening. Thus far, he'd managed not to shout at any of them. But losing his temper here would be just as bad. Or maybe worse, because this wasn't a class. It didn't matter whether people listened or not.

Afterwards, while everyone else stayed to chat and discuss their work, Joe slunk out. Alex watched him go, unsure whether to be disappointed or relieved. Or neither. Because he had zero interest anyway in any kind of entanglement whatsoever. *Zero*.

Chapter Two

Alex was outside, the winter sun warming his back. He was sanding windowsills the old-fashioned way, by hand, with sandpaper. Old paint flaked and crumbled and made his fingers chalky; the red-blonde wood came clear, inch by inch. His arm ached in a good way, and the sea breeze whipped the white dust away. The rasping connection between sandpaper and wood filled his ears.

"I'm really sorry," a young man's voice said behind him. Something about the tone told Alex it wasn't the first thing he'd said. Alex turned, taking off the face-mask he wore to stop himself breathing in paint dust.

Joe stood there in his green snowflake sweater. He was barefoot, a pair of gumboots clutched against his chest, and a fishing rod and bucket in his other hand. The tail of a fish protruded from the top of the bucket. He stood hip-shot, one foot cocked in an odd, balletic pose. His eyes were the colour of dark chocolate and his cheeks were pink. Even under that ugly, too-big sweater Alex could see the lovely lean lines of his shoulders and hips. Joe wobbled, appearing flustered. Well, now. Not so balletic. Pretty devastating all the same.

"Hi," Alex said, heart beating faster, mouth suddenly dry. *I want you. And this is the second time you've blushed at me; maybe you want me too.*

"It's just, I can't get it out by myself," Joe said.

"I'm sorry?"

"The fish hook."

"What?" Alex glanced at the tail of the fish in the bucket. He hadn't been fishing in years. Why would—

Joe wobbled again, stretched out the bucket and rod and the gumboots for balance. "Sorry, do you mind if I sit down?"

He took a limping step and sank onto the concrete slab at the front of the house.

"It's all right, though," he added. "It's not all the way in."

He angled his left foot up, balanced it on his right thigh. Out of his foot stuck the straight metal part of a fish hook, the beginning of the curve still visible. There was a smear of blood where the metal went into the flesh. Metal in flesh. And the curve of a bare foot, sole to the sky.

And a severed foot lay sole up before Alex on a ploughed field. An electric jolt of fear made his skin crawl, his heart race. There'd been an explosion. A bomb. The foot was so close he could see that the skin of the heel was a little cracked. All the toes were still there.

Blood flecked his bare arms, his sweat-soaked shirt. There was wet stuff on his camera and splinters of white. Grit in his mouth and a coppery taste. He checked his body mechanically: arms, legs, feet, hands. He was all right. Birds were screeching, or maybe monkeys, but it was muffled, unreal. He'd stopped to take a picture of women planting rice. Aoife and Khamane had gone on, across the ploughed field. He could see Aoife's white shirt. She lay on the ground, but something was wrong; she seemed to have no legs. He couldn't see Khamane.

He must go to Aoife. This field was supposed to be safe. But if there was one bomb there might be another. He took a step towards her, and as his boot pressed into the earth the fear pulsed through him again, so strong he believed for a split second he'd stepped on another unexploded bomb. He stood gasping, unable to believe that the world was still going on around him. But Aoife was hurt. She was down on the ground. There was no choice. He must go to her. He took another step, and another, clutching his camera, as if that might keep him safe. Someone grabbed his arm; a tiny woman in a black face-mask and conical hat. She was gabbling at him in Laotian, voice high-pitched, the terror in her eyes so naked that he stopped.

And he was staring at a man's bare foot with a fish hook embedded in it. The owner of the foot was the guy who'd been sleeping in the sunroom and he was no threat. He sat there, holding his foot, gazing at Alex open-mouthed, white-faced.

And still Alex was rooted to the ground. He shook his head. *I can't help you*, he wanted to say, but the words wouldn't come. *I would help you if I could.* How long had he been standing here, sandpaper in his hand, gawping at the guy's foot? How long, with his heart pounding and the taste of earth and blood in his mouth?

The guy with the fish hook was talking, but Alex couldn't hear him. He was still deafened by the explosion that had killed Aoife and Khamane. A bomblet from a cluster bomb, decades old. Laos was littered with them. But the field had been cleared. Ploughed. It should have been safe. He'd had to wash splinters of bone from his hair. When he got back to London, he'd opened his camera and found blood still on the lens.

They'd been on assignment for the *Irish Times,* for a piece on how climate change was decimating rural communities around the world. The papers had called the explosion a tragedy, which was ironic considering how many Laotians got blown up in the same way every year, and that was seldom reported. There had been protests outside the American Embassy in London for a time afterwards, because the bombs were all American, left over from the Vietnam war. They'd been blowing people up since the 70s. But Alex had come out of the incident entirely uninjured. Not a scratch. Lucky.

The guy's mouth moved again. Joe, his name was.

"Really, it's not that bad. Maybe I should go. Would that be better?" He took his foot off his thigh and put it down to the ground.

Alex closed his eyes, but that didn't help. Or maybe it did, because when he opened them again, he heard himself say, "I'm sorry."

"No, it's okay. Things like this freak some people out, don't they? I didn't mean to gross you out. It doesn't hurt."

"Uh, yes." Alex didn't know what he was saying yes to, but he had to respond because that's what people did when they had conversations. He closed his eyes again.

Joe said, quietly, "Actually, do you mind if I sit here for a few minutes? Is that okay? I don't know if you remember me, but I saw you the other night at Edith's. I should have said hello, but anyway. I'm Joe. I liked what you said about light as composition."

Alex opened his eyes to see Joe half-turn, gazing up at the house.

Joe said, "Before you moved in, everyone was saying a flash American had bought this place and was going to pull it down. But you're not American, are you? You're Canadian. I suppose people get that wrong all the time, although, actually, I think your accent is quite different. Anyway, if you're sanding windowsills, you're probably not going to demolish this place."

Sanding windows. Yes. Alex had been sanding. His heart was slowing, breath slowing. But he couldn't stop trembling. His right hand hurt. He had the sandpaper in a vicious grip. He let it fall and concentrated on Joe's voice. Joe had a Kiwi accent that made Alex think of straightforward things like sheep and green grass and small country towns. An accent without pretensions. Joe hadn't run away. Not that he could with a hook in his foot.

"This used to be the Addison's place," Joe said. "I used to come here as a kid with my grandma. Mrs. Addison would give me Fox's glacier mints. Did you ever have those? I never ate them, but I liked the polar bear on the wrapper, so I took them anyway. She loved this house. She'd be glad you're doing it up." He seemed to have forgotten the hook in his foot. He looked at Alex as if they'd been sharing secrets. "You okay? I can go now, if you like."

Alex took a deep breath, let it out. "I can't. Sorry. I can't."

"No. No problem," Joe said quickly.

With an effort, Alex tried to think of something sensible to say. "I could take you to a doctor. If you like. In a bit." His voice sounded like it belonged to someone else.

For the first time, Joe seemed nervous. "No, that's okay. I'll try Matire's place."

"Sorry. You picked the wrong person."

Joe gave him a half-smile. Not pitying, but maybe a little sad. "It's fine."

Alex rested his back against the house, and took a deep breath, and then another. A couple of years ago, he would have just helped. Like a competent adult. Like a grown man. He would have taken charge. He would have made the right kind of jokes, been the right mix of matter-of-fact and sympathetic. He would have done whatever was necessary, made Joe a cup of sweet tea and given him a lift home. Probably got his phone number. Maybe got himself invited in, if that was on the cards.

Now, of course, he was a fuck up. The guy with the hook in his foot was calming *him* down. And Joe was half his age, which was its own humiliation. It was sort of acceptable to be a mess at twenty-five; lots of people were. It could even be sexy. But at forty-five it was inexcusable. Not that Alex felt forty-five. He felt simultaneously about ninety and about nine. His hands wouldn't stop shaking. He was like a grotesque hybrid of a palsied old man and a kid freaking out.

Since coming to Kahawai Bay, things had improved. He'd been sleeping better, feeling better, hadn't yelled at anyone. And now this.

Suddenly, he wanted rid of Joe. Why had he brought his problem here? Why the hell did he have a hook in his foot in the first place? What kind of idiot carried his boots along a beach where careless fuckwits drop their fish hooks? Rage was washing over him.

Oh fuck.

"I'll be back," Alex managed through gritted teeth, and strode away down the grassy path to the sea.

Please, let there be no one on the beach. Let there be no one fishing. Let no one drop a fucking fish hook on the ground anywhere in a ten-mile radius or I'll brain the fucking bastard with a rock.

At the beach, he took the hill path. Some hikers were coming down, but he hurried past them, avoiding eye contact, and they didn't speak. On top of the cliffs, there was nothing but the wind, and the gulls riding the currents over a hundred-metre drop. In the distance, he could see the South Island, blue mountains across the sparkling sea. The anger was ebbing. The wind tore his body warmth away, and he felt cold and small. He wanted to be home, safe in the afternoon sun on the Chesterfield. But he'd left Joe there so he couldn't go back. Not yet. A headache pulsed in his left temple.

Ah, God, why did it have to be the young handsome guy I freaked out in front of? Why couldn't it have been some crusty old codger with a beard like steel wool?

Well, because that was life. The divine comedy. And sometimes it was so funny, the tears ran down his face and he gasped for breath.

After a while, he remembered the kind, plump face of his therapist in London, her rather posh English accent, her voice always calm, always quiet. After nearly a year, he'd grown sick of listening to her, and sicker still of listening to himself. Now, he often thought of her at times like this. He tried to relax in the way she'd suggested. Tried telling himself those sensible things you were supposed to tell yourself: everybody can have a bad day, it doesn't mean you're back at square one, it's a long road, what doesn't kill you makes you stronger, you're doing fine.

Wouldn't it be nice if they felt true?

Probably the story would get around that the Canadian guy who'd bought Addison's and seemed so nice, was actually pretty fucking weird. And Matire wouldn't want her kids showing him how to eat *kina*, and there would be no more invitations to art groups or people coming to check the water tank out of a sense of neighbourliness. It was pathetic to mind, because what did it matter what these people thought? And yet it did. Because he liked it here, with these people who thought quilting was an art-form and yet had original Warhols in their living rooms, and who cared about herons and not what kind of sweater you wore. He wanted to stay and feel safe here at the edge of the world, and have ordinary good things in his life.

He had no idea of the time because he'd left his phone at home, but eventually the sun began to set, and he grew so cold that nothing else mattered. He stumbled down the stony hill track, up the grassy valley one. The concrete step was empty. Joe had gone. And Alex had said 'I'll be back' like the Terminator. And of course, had *not* come back. So that was another mark against him, another unreliable act. He opened the unlocked front door, resigning himself to a night of hell, and trod on a piece of white paper. Wearily, he turned on the light and picked up the paper, ready for questions, apologies, or recriminations, but it wasn't a note at all. It was a series of pencil drawings, in panels like a comic strip.

The first panel showed a young man going fishing, rod over his shoulder, bucket in hand. Joe had drawn himself skinnier and uglier than in real life, like a stick insect with soulful eyes, a big nose, and prominent Adam's apple. He'd exaggerated his posture, lampooning his own lankiness and awkwardness. He wore the snowflake sweater. In the next panel, he stood on a rocky ledge, wind blowing his hair, line in the sea. He caught a fish, put it in his bucket, and began to walk home. But he stopped, sat down on a rock. His ill-fitting boots had chafed holes in his socks and given him blisters. *Ah, so that's why he'd taken them off.* Joe carried his boots instead, picking his way barefoot along the beach.

In the next panel, a fish hook was wedged between two stones, barbed point flashing in the sun, Joe's bare foot poised above it. At the last moment, Joe noticed it, and leapt aside. He picked up the hook, frowning, stowed it in his bucket. He went on, glancing up into a valley where a small square house faced the sun. A man was working outside the house, sanding windowsills. Although he remained a distant figure, it was clearly Alex, same hooded sweatshirt, same haircut; short at the sides, longer on top. The next panel showed Joe's face close up, a thought cloud above his head. In the cloud was a picture of Alex talking to the art group, laptop showing a tiny approximation of the Cartier-Bresson photo of a woman on a stairway. Joe really *had* been paying attention.

But in the next panel, Joe sighed, and turned away, cheeks hatched. The implication was clear: too shy to say hello. Joe trudged on, posture exaggeratedly dejected, boots and bucket trailing on the ground behind him. He left the beach, went past a field with an old horse grazing. Then down a long driveway, a black cloud appearing above his head. He put the bucket by the front door of a tiny, ramshackle house that appeared to be roofed with leaves, and went in, closing the door behind him. The final panel showed the fish, upside-down in the bucket, dead eye staring at nothing.

The drawings were beautifully done, stylised but exact, leaping with life.

At the very bottom of the page was a symbol like pi gone wrong. Alex frowned at it before realising it was initials: JT.

Alex stood in the open doorway, scanning the pictures again. So, if Joe hadn't trodden on the fish hook, he'd never have introduced himself. And that was—sad?

Alex read it a third time. The staring eye of the dead fish at the end definitely felt like a summary of how things would have ended up if Joe had not stepped on the fish hook: blank, empty, lifeless. So, since Joe *had* trodden on the hook, what was the alternative ending?

Alex looked again at the panel in which Joe sighed and turned away, cheeks hatched. Was he really so shy? He was brave enough to ask for help when he needed it, and brave enough to draw these pictures and leave them behind for Alex to find. And he'd done it with a hook in his foot. His lines were confident and economical. The way he caricatured himself was masterful; he was clearly used to doing it. He might attend an art group with old ladies, but he drew like a professional illustrator.

Alex had opened his door feeling like shit and expecting to feel like shit for days, if not weeks. Now, he was almost smiling. His hands were trembling again, but for a different reason. Because Joe seemed to be saying, 'I'm not sorry I stood on a fish hook, and I don't mind that you acted like a lunatic, because at least we met.'

I wonder where he lives? Where is this house with leaves for a roof? Surely, that's artistic licence? Is a bit flirtatious or is that wishful thinking? Perhaps it's just kind.

I have to see him again.

But not now. He couldn't face anything else today. Not even a sympathetic New Zealander with a sensible accent and a shy smile.

He gazed at the drawing in his hand and wondered, suddenly, whether this was actually happening. It seemed unlikely, like something from a dream. Alex's real life was going on without him in London. Right now, the genuine Alex Cox was heading to the Dorchester to photograph the newest face from Hollywood.

He drank a glass of water and dragged himself to bed. On the bedside table, he put the comic strip. Perhaps, in the morning, it would be gone.

Chapter Three

The next morning, Alex walked along the beach to the art gallery. He arrived as Juleke was opening the front door. Today, she wore a camouflage print fleece with her gumboots, and looked more like a backwoods hunter than a gallery owner.

"Hello!" she said. "Well! Everyone in the art group hopes you'll come again! Now, are you a customer today, or is this a social call?"

"You know Joe, from the art group? He did me a favour yesterday. I wanted to thank him. Know where I could find him?"

"Gave you a fish, did he? People often do that around here."

"A drawing. He left it for me to find."

"Clever, isn't he? Very talented. Did he speak to you? Because, if so, you can count yourself lucky. He's all right once he knows you, though."

"Actually, he talked more than I did," Alex said.

"Really?" She laughed. "That'll be a first. He must like you."

"Sometimes I don't say much myself."

She nodded. "We all have our days, don't we? Me, I talk too much. But that's all right. Takes all sorts, doesn't it? Joe lives up the Makara Road; it's a ten-minute walk. Tui Glen, it's called. It's got a tui on the letter box—you know the bird with the white tuft under its chin? So, you can't miss it. But he's at work at the moment; I happen to know because his car wouldn't start and I gave him a ride in. I'll tell him you're looking for him, though, if I see him. Or you could go around later. Frank's giving him a ride home and he usually comes back around four. Try then."

"Thanks."

"I tell you what; want to see one of Joe's paintings? I've got one in. It's good. I guarantee you'll want it."

Joe's painting showed pale blue sky, half a dozen seagulls tumbling across it, coming in to land. The gulls were stylised into a pattern of white and red and grey, and the whole thing had a cheerful, early morning feel. They weren't noble wind-riding gulls; their peevish red beaks and paddle-feet gave them a droll look, and yet the angles of wings and heads and bodies all fitted together into perfect harmony. They were at once real birds and a representation of agile, squabbling joy. The colours weren't over-bright. On the contrary, Joe had used a subtle palette—burgundy, dove grey, duck-egg-blue—that gave the whole thing a mid-century feel. It was fresh and new, but the viewer travelled in time to see it.

Alex had been to hundreds of art galleries, thousands of shows. He didn't often buy, but this was charming. It would be perfect in the house in Kahawai Bay. And not a mandala or metal bikini in sight. Juleke stood at his elbow, gazing at it too. He'd gone to such lengths to avoid coming in here, and now he was going to buy something. Not out of a sense of obligation, but because he really wanted it. Would he have wanted it if the artist hadn't been Joe? Yes. It was that good.

Juleke was nodding. "Beautiful, eh? What do you think? Will you take it?"

"Yes, thanks, I will."

"I can get it framed, if you like. Something plain? Black? Not too thick?"

"All right. How much?"

"For you, including the framing, four hundred dollars."

Alex frowned. The painting was quite big. "That's not enough. A frame alone…"

"It's mate's rates, isn't it? Joe would kill me if I charged full price to a local."

"Am I a local yet? You're under-charging. I'd happily pay more."

"If Joe was here, he'd probably give it to you for nothing and that won't help me pay the mortgage. You give me four hundred and we'll all be happy."

And with that, he had to be content. He took a photo of the picture with his phone and walked home. He was opening the front door when he realised he hadn't even glanced at anything else in the gallery, hadn't asked about Juleke's work at all. He'd have to go back one day soon. He sat at the kitchen table and contemplated the photo of the seagull picture. It had a carefree, holiday feel, like a 1950s British Rail poster advertising trips to the seaside.

He zoomed in and found a signature in pencil, silvery grey against pale blue, J. Taylor. Now he had a surname, he Googled 'Joe Taylor Wellington artist', and clicked on images, hoping equally for photos of the artist, or more of his pictures. What he got was a website offering page after page of comics. All in the same style as the one lying on his bedside table, but in colour.

Joe's comics were set in the small town of New Erewhon and featured an eclectic cast of real people, animals, and anthropomorphised objects. Edith made an appearance, along with a talking fish, and a bucket having an existential crisis. There was a knight in armour who was a caricature of Joe himself with a pot on his head, riding an old white horse around the country roads. The horse, named Blue, sometimes hung out in Joe's leaf-roofed house and quoted Kierkegaard when Joe was sad. The horse smoked marijuana in secret behind its stall, and then craved oats, which Joe couldn't afford.

For Alex, comics were a childhood thing: Superman, Batman, Mickey Mouse. As an adult, they'd barely been on his radar. But as he read, the world Joe had created began to grow on him. And when he reached a storyline with Joe's green snowflake sweater as a character in its own right, he laughed out loud. In the comic, Joe treated the sweater carelessly, not realising that at night it came to life and roamed the dark hillsides, causing mischief and performing mysterious rituals.

No one had any money in Joe's comics. Their lives were not glamorous. Characters sometimes died or got eaten or were simply thrown away. The remaining characters suffered from ennui or thwarted love affairs. Their ambitions were often ridiculous. Occasionally, Joe put superheroes into his storylines. They wore spandex suits and tried to do good, but they were all hopeless, with useless talents, or so pompous no one could stand them.

But a thread of joy or hope ran through all of Joe's stories. Ingenuity and kindness always won through, and people were seldom alone unless they wanted to be. In the bleakest storylines, there was always a suggestion of redemption in the final panel. Even as the bucket concluded that life wasn't worth living, another bucket was washed up on the shore behind him, weakly calling for help. The storylines were so tight, the art so accomplished, and the characters so nuanced, that they drew Alex in to a world he didn't want to leave.

Defining Joe from his comics was more difficult, because while his website's About page stated that they were semi-autobiographical, his flights of fancy made it difficult to know which things had really happened and which had not. Quite a lot of the older comics had the 'Joe' character pining after a beautiful mermaid, and Alex's heart sank, because that seemed to signal pretty clearly where the real Joe's romantic interests might lie.

But the mermaid tired of Joe, and Joe met the Prince Frog, a charmer who became crueler and more frog-like with every kiss. Of course, it was a work of fiction. Of course, it was none of Alex's business. Of course, a comic in which a sweater came alive and horses talked philosophy was hardly proof of anything. But all the same, Alex couldn't help lingering over the panels in which Joe lay in bed with the Prince Frog, or tried to hold his webbed hand.

Eventually, Alex tore himself away from the world of New Erewhon. He found that there was a book, a collection from a publisher called *Earth's End Comics*. He bought it, and fetched the pencilled comic strip Joe had left behind, Alex's own personal piece of New Erewhon. Perhaps he could reciprocate with a print of a photograph. There was a dark room at the studio. He knew exactly which image he'd choose.

* * *

In real life, the roof of Joe's house was made of tiles, but covered in so much moss that it did look like leaves. The house, at the foot of a huge hill, was very small, similar in size and era to Alex's. The walls were wooden weatherboard, painted pale yellow and overlaid with green algae. Alex parked on the road and walked down the long driveway. An old white horse in an adjoining field flicked its ears and ambled towards the house alongside him. Was it called Blue?

Joe's white Honda with the one red door was parked beside the house. Next to the car, a concrete garage had been built against the bare hillside that loomed over the house. The garage door was open, showing a heap of driftwood, a pile of bigger logs stacked against a wall, and several bales of hay.

The air smelled of wood smoke. Someone was home. Was it Joe? Did he live alone? Heart beating faster, Alex knocked on the door.

The old horse thrust its head through the wires of the fence and tore at the longer grass at the side of the driveway. Although the time was only four thirty, the hill meant the house was already in shade, and probably had been for hours. It was cold and damp, chilling Alex to the bone. No wonder Joe used to seek out the afternoon warmth in Mrs. Addison's sunroom.

Alex knocked again. No answer. Juleke had said Joe was shy. Joe had said it himself in his drawing. Maybe he was hiding.

Alex pushed the envelope with the photograph he'd printed under the front door. On the back of the photo he'd written: *Sorry about yesterday. Thanks for the comic* and his name and phone number. He'd taken a couple of steps away from the house when he heard the door opening and turned.

Joe stood in the doorway, holding the envelope. He wore his grey coat, buttoned up, as if he was about to go out. He was looking down at the envelope, so all Alex could see was his hair; he must have washed it, because it was glossy as mahogany.

"Sorry to keep you waiting. I thought you were someone else," Joe said to the ground.

"Hi. Look, I wanted to say sorry for yesterday. I sometimes can't deal with…situations like that. Hope you're okay."

"I'm fine." Joe flipped a corner of the envelope backwards and forwards with his thumb. His gaze skittered over Alex, up the driveway to the road, then back to the envelope. In this light, his eyes were black and shiny as wet tar.

"Your picture meant a lot to me," Alex said. "I thought you'd be pretty pissed."

"Oh, no." Joe stared at his feet.

"You draw very well."

"Oh, no. I mean, thanks."

"That's a print, of a photo. I wanted to reciproca–"

"Thanks." Joe spoke so fast he cut Alex off. Then he frowned and blushed and said, "Sorry. Thanks."

"I hope you like it," Alex said.

Joe made no move to open the envelope. He seemed quite different than the guy who'd sat and talked calmly about sanding windowsills and Fox's glacier mints. Perhaps he was hoping Alex wasn't going to do anything else crazy.

Alex added, "Well, I guess I'll see you round? Don't be shy. I hope, if you want to come and say hi, you'll come."

Joe shot him a glance that was almost irritated, like he'd been caught out. *You put it in the comic you gave me*, Alex wanted to say. But then he imagined Joe, on the beach path, seeing his house again, not coming over again. *Don't be shy* was a dumb thing to say to a shy person who doesn't know you very well.

"Why don't you come tonight? I'll make you dinner," Alex said, surprising himself.

Joe's eyes widened in astonishment, lips parting. He looked Alex straight in the eye for the first time. Then he went scarlet down to his neck, and ducked his head again. "Oh. Uh, are you sure?"

"I'd love to make you dinner. I hope I didn't freak you out yesterday."

"You didn't."

"The thing is, something happened to me. I was on an assignment. In South-East Asia. In Laos. I was sick of commercial stuff. I was moving into photojournalism. But the people I was with—a journalist and our interpreter—died. They were killed. There was an unexploded bomb, and one of them stepped on it. It's not that I knew them well, but…but…and now sometimes I can't deal with things like…your foot and…uh…"

Khamane's severed foot popped into his mind and he lost the thread. Sweat was pricking out down his back and in his armpits. Why on earth was he trying to explain it to someone he'd barely met, to someone he'd just invited for dinner? He could taste blood.

"I know worse things happen to people every day, but ever since it happened, sometimes I…I just can't."

Joe was watching him now.

It was Alex's turn to avert his eyes. "I was ashamed I couldn't help you. I'm usually all right, these days." The image of the severed foot hovered in his mind. He kept trying to push it away; it kept being flung back, like a piece of driftwood on an incoming tide.

He'd planned on saying *sorry* and *thanks* and maybe *call me, if you like*. Hadn't planned on saying all this other stuff. He took a deep breath and forced himself to make eye contact again.

"Anyway, if you don't want to come over, it's fine. I won't be offended. I know you don't know me," Alex said.

Joe bent his head again, contemplating his feet, as if he was going to refuse. "Dinner sounds nice, if you're sure." He shot a look at Alex from under his hair. Not smiling, but pleased. Interested. Still astonished.

And he'd said yes. Alex felt the tingle he got when going through shots at the end of a long day and realising he'd taken something special.

"Great," Alex said. "About seven? I can come and get you, if you like. I heard you were having car trouble."

A silver-grey Mazda turned in at driveway and Joe jerked his head up. The car bumped towards the house, coming too fast. The white horse shied away from it, catching its ears on the wire and making the whole fence rattle. As the car pulled up, Alex could see a young blond guy driving; he was good-looking, Joe's age, hair sleek and undercut, wearing a sweatshirt with a plaid pattern printed on it in silver.

"I'll leave you to it," Alex said. Because of course a guy as handsome as Joe would have other people hanging around. Of course, other people could see past his bowed head and ugly sweaters.

"Hi, Jophiel," said the young blond man, getting out of the car.

"Cut it out, Sean," Joe said.

Alex had been intending on walking back to his car. The tension in Joe's voice made him pause.

"Hi," Sean said to Alex, in a *who the hell are you* tone. He said to Joe, "So, what's up?"

"Sean, you can't just—" Joe said.

"Aw." Sean made a mock sad face. "C'mon. Don't moan. Wanna go to town?"

"No," Joe said, with utter finality.

"My place?" Sean said.

"I don't want to," Joe said. "I told you."

"You can drive," Sean said, with the air of one conferring a favour, and threw his keys to Joe.

Joe fumbled the catch, dropped the envelope, and had to pick the keys up off the front step to toss them back. "Sean, can you just go?"

"Why? Got a date?"

Joe opened his mouth and closed it again, reddening. Sean's eyes widened with real surprise, then narrowed, hardening. Alex glanced at Joe. Was having dinner together a date? He wasn't sure himself. Was Joe embarrassed because Sean had got it right, or because he'd got it wrong? When Alex glanced back to Sean, Sean's eyes had widened again in mockery; he looked Alex up and down.

"You're kidding," Sean said.

"I told you not to come," Joe said. "I *told* you."

"Yeah." Sean was glaring at Alex. "Jesus, Jophiel. He's about a hundred."

"At least, I'm old enough to recognise a loser when I see one," Alex said. His voice came out perfect, bored and dismissive. He realised, with some surprise, that he *felt* dismissive. Whoever this idiot was, Joe wasn't interested. Also, this idiot was a guy, and he'd clearly had some sort of relationship with Joe. So that was pretty conclusive. Good.

Sean huffed in mock outrage. "Bloody hell, it's Bryan Adams. Joe, you are so lame."

"Sean, go *away*," Joe said fiercely.

"God, you're pathetic," Sean said. "You were only ever a pity fuck, you know."

"Fuck you," Joe said under his breath at Sean's retreating back.

Sean got in his car, reversed into the garage wall, sped back up the driveway and was gone towards Wellington with a nasty dent in his rear fender.

Joe's knees seemed to give. He hid his face in his hands and hunched against the doorframe. "Oh, God, I'm sorry."

"'Bryan Adams'? Well, I've had worse."

"Oh, God," Joe groaned, position becoming more foetal. "I'm really, really sorry."

Alex ducked his head, trying to read Joe's expression, which of course was impossible. But Joe didn't seem upset as such. He was just suffering an agony of embarrassment.

"Put it like this," Alex said. "That's your cringe quota over for the year. So now you can relax. Nothing that bad will happen again anytime soon, will it?"

Joe laughed, sort of, but stayed curled up in the doorway.

"Was he the 'Prince Frog'?" Alex asked.

Joe took his hands away from his face. "You read my comic."

"Yep. I bought one of your paintings today. The seagulls. You signed it. So, I Googled you, found your website."

"Uh, thanks for buying a picture."

"*Was* he the Prince Frog? Got nastier the more you kissed him?"

"Sean was never…" Joe paused, as if deciding something. "He was never my boyfriend."

"No?"

"I would never go out with someone like that."

Meaning, a guy? Or meaning, a dickhead? Alex could certainly understand why Joe would want to distance himself from a charmer like Sean.

"Neither would I. You know, I really liked your comic. I loved the stories about your snowflake sweater. And Edith in New York. Does she know?"

"Oh, yes. I asked her." Joe picked up the envelope and began playing with the corner again. "You know what? I Googled you, too. After you came to art group."

"Is that right?" *So, you were curious about me. And you probably already knew everything I just told you about Laos.*

"You met Alan Moore, didn't you? You took his picture."

"Oh, the comics guy? With the beard and the hair? Of course, you like comics. You like his?"

Joe gaped at him, wordless, and Alex could see that had been a really stupid question.

"Why don't you come over now?" Alex said. "Tell me about comics while I cook. I can give you a lift, if you like. I parked on the road."

"Um."

"I might remember an anecdote about Alan Moore."

"Okay, thanks," Joe said. He added, as if reassuring himself, "It's not far, anyway."

"We can walk if you like," Alex said. He remembered Sean tossing his keys to Joe. "Or you can drive."

Joe gave him a look that made his heart turn over and his balls tighten.

"I think I trust you," Joe said.

In the car, Joe took the photograph of the sunroom out of the envelope. A shaft of copper sunlight lay across the old Chesterfield, the doorway framing the red-washed hill opposite. The moth-eaten paper lantern glowed on the floor like the ghost of a jack-o-lantern, sending unexpected rays of light across floor and wall. It was a warm, inviting image. *Come in*, it seemed to say. *The door is always open. Lie down. Rest.* Alex was pleased with it.

"Like it?"

"It's beautiful." Joe was staring. Not at the picture. At Alex.

"Know why I chose that picture?" Alex said.

"You saw me there. Didn't you?"

"I arrived before the estate agent. Checked the place out. Did you hear me slam my car door?"

"That was you?"

"Yep."

"That was my big secret. Mrs. Addison's spare key."

"Sorry. Ruined your afternoon naps, haven't I?"

"It was so warm. If I'd had a bad night's sleep I'd just…you're not annoyed, are you?"

"Why would I be? You were a good advertisement. Made me want the place all the more. That old Chesterfield's better than sleeping pills, eh?"

"That old—? Is it some kind of antique?"

"Chesterfield is Canadian slang. It means your grandma's couch."

"You're kidding! You have a word for that?"

Alex glanced away from the road. Joe smiling at him was the best thing he'd seen in months.

Back at home, Alex offered tea, because there was no wine or beer in the house. Joe sat at the kitchen table and accepted as if tea was a perfect aperitif.

One-to-one and sure of his welcome, Joe was easy company. If he blushed easily, he smiled easily, too, and didn't rush to fill silences. At first it felt a bit of a novelty to be with someone under thirty who wasn't forever checking his phone, but of course there was no reception in Kahawai Bay. Joe didn't seem bothered. He pulled a sketchbook out of his coat pocket and drew, stopping to talk if spoken to, but absorbing himself in his drawing when the silence lengthened. Watching Joe sketching was unexpectedly relaxing. It was like seeing flames flickering in a fireplace, always different, always the same. It gave the conversation an effortless, rambling quality, as if they'd known each other for years.

Joe had a part-time job at an artist's supply shop in town. He owned the house he lived in; it had been left to him by his grandmother, who had also bequeathed him old Blue. Not having to pay rent or a mortgage meant Joe could spend a lot of time making comics. He sometimes picked up commissions, mainly illustrating educational resources for schools, or did artwork for book covers and magazine-style websites. He sold drawings and prints online and at a gallery in town that specialised in comics and tattoo-style art. But he didn't care about money, except to keep body and soul together and buy hay for Blue.

Alex began to cook spaghetti bolognaise. He would have liked to make something more impressive, but there wasn't much in the cupboards. Joe said spaghetti sounded great. Avoiding carbs had probably never entered his head. Joe mentioned a couple of comics artists, but kept turning the conversation back to other things.

Alex said, "You won't bore me. Tell me some more about this Jim Woodring guy."

Alex's laptop was on the table, and Joe started finding pictures for him to look at, pointing out what he liked, or didn't like, or hoped to emulate. When discussing comics, Joe forgot to be shy. He contradicted Alex without apologising. He said, "I *have* to lend you some comics." He pushed his hair off his face and his features leapt into focus: smooth brow, coffee-dark eyes, strong nose, clean jawline. He had a pale scar down the very middle of his bottom lip.

The scar caught the light, a white seam on pink. Slightly raised. Alex had a sudden, electric vision of Joe kneeling before him, mouth around his dick. He could almost *feel* the scar catching on the head, just a little. Could almost feel Joe's hair like silk beneath his hand. The kitchen was suddenly too bright and sweltering hot. He was longing to ask Joe if he could take his photograph, but something kept stopping him. *Trust the instinct, because he'll say no.* Alex tried instead to focus on the gaudy hallucinogenic animals Joe was currently displaying on the computer screen.

Alex showed Joe some photos. Joe had a good eye, although he critiqued photos in a surprising way, valuing atmosphere over narrative. He noticed things about lighting that most beginners didn't pick up.

After dinner, Alex said, "Why did he call you Jophiel?"

"It's my name," Joe said to his empty spaghetti bowl. "Awful, isn't it? It's after an angel. Mum's a bit New Age. We lived in a commune until I was fourteen. Mind you, my best friend was called Blessing, and her brother was Windroval, so I suppose I got off lightly." He looked across the table at Alex. "Don't call me it, will you? I don't like it."

Alex had known a number of people in New York and London who'd changed their names to be more noticeable, more unusual, more unforgettable. It seemed telling that Joe would go about life in the opposite way.

Later, he took Joe home.

"Thanks, it was awesome," Joe said in the dark car. "Thanks for the photograph, too. It's amazing."

Before Laos, Alex would probably have gone in for a kiss, because, why not? Now, he felt very conscious of his age and his many weaknesses. He was hardly love's young dream.

"It was awesome, eh? We should do it again," he said.

Joe opened the car door and the light went on. He shot Alex a heart-stopping smile, got out, closed the car door and was gone into his tiny yellow house. Alex drove home. He tided the kitchen, trying to ignore his incipient hard-on. He closed the browser windows and turned off the laptop. He brushed his teeth and got into bed. But there was no ignoring it now. He said *shit* under his breath, tugged down his shorts and took himself in hand.

He thought of Joe, lying asleep on the Chesterfield in the sunroom. Joe waking, seeing Alex standing in the doorway. Joe undoing the fly of his paint-spattered pants, staring at Alex as he did it. Joe pulling off his clothes. Joe's limber young body, long lean muscles, hard dick leaking onto his flat stomach. *Ah, yes.* Alex mentally fast-forwarded. Joe lying on his back at the edge of the sofa, sunlight gilding his body. Joe with his knees hooked over Alex's shoulders. Joe crying out as Alex thrust into his tight ass, perfectly lubed and prepared by the magic of erotic fantasy. Joe pushing up against him, pleading for more, making desperate noises, begging to be fucked…

Alex came hard and fast, and saw stars the glow of the bedside lamp. Now that he'd come, his bones were turning into limp spaghetti. Too tired to get out of bed, he tugged off his T-shirt, wiped away the come with it, and tossed it on the floor. He switched off the light.

He thought of the real Joe, flashing him a smile and closing the car door. The bed had never felt emptier. If only Joe was still here, sleepy and affectionate in Alex's arms, warming the whole world with his presence.

Physically sated, if not precisely happy, Alex fell asleep.

Chapter Four

Alex started to see Joe two or three times a week. Of course, it was silly and adolescent to frequent places Joe might go, but he did it all the same. And it was easy to meet by chance in a place the size of Makara Beach. He might find Joe giving Matire's kids a plodding horseback ride on old Blue. Or fishing off the rocks, or sketching. Once, Alex bumped into him at the nearest supermarket in suburban Karori, where Joe was buying cheap, sensible things like pasta and beans.

Sometimes, Joe had 'comics people' over, and invariably took them down to the beach. Alex met a few of them: Rawiri, who drew epic Māori mythology-inspired fantasies and who greeted Alex with a hongi, the traditional Māori pressing together of noses. Bella, who drew threatening, wordless, scratchy black-and-white comics, and who was even shyer than Joe. And Oliver, who was into autobiographical anguish and made comics about watching too much porn, losing a joint in his mother's car, and failing at job interviews.

Alex gathered, from these meetings, that Joe was something of a celebrity in the Wellington comics scene. Joe had a book out, and another collection planned, and was generous with his time, discussing other people's comics at length, and showing tricks he'd learned with the drawing software they all used. With the comics people, Joe talked about zine markets or comics meet-ups; he teased Oliver about the way he drew girls' breasts, and Rawiri about his love of superheroes.

One day, Alex met Joe and Rawiri on the beach and invited them back for coffee. Rawiri wore his long black hair pulled back in a bun. He was older than Joe, in his early thirties, married with kids. Māori tattoos swirled up both well-muscled forearms. More tattoos snaked up the sides of his neck. His eyes, a lighter brown than Joe's and slightly protuberant, missed nothing. Alex felt as if he was meeting Joe's dad. He could tell Rawiri was making up his mind about him.

Rawiri pointed to the painting of the seagulls, now framed and hanging on the wall above the kitchen table. "That's your work, my friend," he said to Joe. "Nice. Very nice."

"Thanks," Joe muttered, squirming the way he did when complimented, and staring into his coffee.

"Ah, you kumara!" Rawiri said. "Where did you learn to be so shy? Did you not do your best work? Then own it! That's what I tell my kids."

"It is my best." Joe glanced at Alex and smiled.

"Well, then!" Rawiri said to Alex. "There's a whakatauki, Alex, a saying: kāore te kumara e kōrero mō tōna ake reka. The kumara—that's the sweet potato—doesn't boast about how sweet it is. Normally it's a lesson in humility, but in this case the kumara is too shy for his own good."

"Ra, don't," Joe said.

"You see?" Rawiri said, holding out his hands. "Alex, you've lived in London. New York. I bet you've seen a lot of the best art, eh? A lot of the finest artists. And yet, you bought this picture. A world-class photographer buys your work, Joe Taylor, and still you won't stand tall. What's going on, eh?"

"I'm hardly world-class," Alex said.

Rawiri threw his hands up, laughing. "You too?" He looked from Alex to Joe and back again, grinning. "You deserve each other."

"He's right, Joe," Alex said. "It's a great picture. You should be proud of it."

"It's not that I'm ashamed," Joe said to the table-top. "I just hate being in the spotlight."

"Yes, but why?" Rawiri asked. "Aren't we all friends here?"

"Okay." Joe grinned at him, suddenly. "Help me break out of my comfort zone. Give me more compliments."

"Ah, that's better," Rawiri said. "I'll make an exhibitionist of you yet!"

Joe shook his head, still smiling. "Never going to happen. You know, when I was at school I used to make mistakes deliberately so I wouldn't win some stupid certificate and have to go on stage to get it."

"And yet you put your comics out there for everyone to read. I reckon you like attention as much as the next guy."

"Maybe. But it has to be the right sort," Joe said.

* * *

Joe wore the green snowflake sweater because someone from art group had given it to him. And yes, because it was warm and his house was freezing. In any case, Alex had started liking the sweater, because it was part of Joe's universe, and the idea of it living a wild and mysterious life of its own made him smile. Joe called it a jumper, not a sweater, and was always saying things like 'I found a dead possum by my back door this morning. I think the jumper did it. Do you think it's territorial?' or 'the jumper's been breaking into people's garages to steal paint. What do you think it wants it for?'.

Alex quickly learned that the surest way to make Joe laugh was to enter into these fantasies. Joe loved ridiculous, playful ideas: sweaters stealing paint to daub snowflake patterns on other people's laundry, a tribe of possums who thought Joe was an undertaker since he always buried their dead, mermaids trying to invent an underwater hair dryer. Cruel humour made Joe uncomfortable. He didn't like to laugh at people. But to be teased by Joe felt like a rare, gentle honour.

One night, a southerly storm brought winds howling straight up from Antarctica. The next morning, Alex met Joe on the beach and suggested a trip to the south coast. Since Alex had arrived in Wellington he'd been waiting for a big southerly so he could photograph the huge seas people kept telling him about. Waves ten metres high thundered across Cook Strait, if the locals were telling the truth. Today, conditions were interesting; the rain had blown over, the swell was up, the sun came out fitfully through low cloud, and Alex had nowhere else to be. Joe offered to drive.

It wasn't far to the south coast, mainly down quiet, semi-rural or suburban roads. Joe drove in total silence. No radio, no chat, giving his full attention to the sparse traffic. Alex didn't mind. It was enough to be with Joe. When they reached the south coast, Alex understood how sheltered they'd been at Makara, and driving through the suburbs. Now the wind buffeted the car so hard it wobbled. The waves were cobalt monsters, maned with white, flinging themselves at the land. Seaweed and driftwood littered the road.

Joe parked where the road petered out into stony beach. The sea roared and seethed to the left, bare hills towered above them to the right. Walking along the narrow track above the beach felt like skirting an abyss. The ground trembled with the fury of the sea.

Over the thunder of the breakers, Joe said, into Alex's ear, "Don't get too close, okay? There are freak waves sometimes." He gazed into Alex's eyes, part smiling, part serious, making Alex's heart skip and race. "Wouldn't want your nice camera to get wet."

Despite the wind, and the cold, and the spatters of icy spray, the photography gods were smiling. Or perhaps it was Joe's presence that made Alex feel especially alert. It was only after a couple of hours in the zone that Alex realised Joe had not once asked if he was nearly finished. Nor had Joe hung around looking patient, or trying to seem interested. In fact, Joe wasn't even watching him anymore. Joe had found a rock to shelter behind, and was leaning on it, drawing.

"Had enough?" Alex said. His fingers were numb.

"Twenty minutes?"

On the way back to the car, Joe kept rubbing his left shoulder. He saw Alex noticing.

"The cold makes it ache," Joe explained. "Should've gone when you said."

"Did you break it?"

"Yeah. Car crash."

"Sorry to hear it."

"No, it's okay. It was ages ago. Two years now."

They carried on for another fifty metres, feet crunching on the stones of the path.

Joe said, "Don't ever drink and drive, okay?"

"I don't. I don't drink these days anyway. Is that what happened?"

"Yeah. Not me. The guy who hit me. He was four times the limit. Speeding too."

"Ah, shit. I'm sorry, Joe."

Alex remembered Joe sitting on his front step with the fish hook in his foot, talking calmly about things that didn't matter. If he'd been in an accident, perhaps someone had talked like that to him. Was that where he'd got the idea? If so, it was even sweeter than Alex had first thought.

Joe gave an awkward, one-shouldered shrug. "No, it's all right. I was lucky. Not to die, I mean."

"I guess that makes two of us."

Alex thought the conversation was over, but back at the car, in the moment of quiet as they closed the doors on the wind, Joe said, "Are you angry about what happened to you?"

Alex glanced at him in surprise. Not because of the question, but at the sudden realisation that no one else, barring the therapist, had ever asked him that. Joe was staring ahead, out of the windshield, at the waves.

"Yeah. I try not to be, but, yeah. You know why I don't drink? Because I started drinking too much. And then, the last two times, I ended up shouting at someone. That's not who I want to be."

Joe nodded, rubbing his shoulder.

"Were you angry about the crash?" Alex asked.

"Yes. At first. I kind of hated the guy who hit me. It felt like a brush with evil. Not deliberate evil, just stupid, thoughtless, arrogant evil. You know what I mean? But after a while it felt pointless to go on being angry." He paused. "Of course, it's easier for me. I haven't got, you know, what you've got."

"Post-traumatic stress disorder."

"Yeah, that." Joe shot him a shy look. "I'm sorry about what happened to you."

Alex wasn't sure whether to smile or burst into tears. "Yeah, well. Thanks. Me too."

He managed to glance at Joe. Joe gave him the tiniest of smiles. Alex hoped Joe wasn't going to start giving him platitudes or trying to cheer him up. Today had been the best day in a long line of good days. He still didn't think he'd be able to bear it if Joe began talking about silver linings.

Joe started the car. "Life's hard sometimes, isn't it?"

You make it easier, Alex wanted to say, but he felt too raw and the words too risky.

"I hope you don't mind that I don't talk when I drive," Joe said, as he backed out and turned the car. "Ever since the crash I've been kind of a nervous driver. I need to concentrate."

"Want me to drive home?"

"No, actually. I'm worse as a passenger. There's something about not being in control."

Alex frowned. "You've let me drive you. I took you to work that time. And to my place."

"Didn't you notice me flinching at intersections?"

"No, I didn't. You hide it very well."

"So do you," Joe said.

That evening, alone at home, Alex assessed the shots he'd taken. The best ones came when he'd been waiting for Joe. The light had changed again. The sea had become a torrent of pure, glinting power, gnawing at the rocks. The fold of hill he'd got in shot was massive, unyielding, just as potent in a totally different way. Alex got the shiver on the back of his neck, the hairs standing up on his arms. He felt like a photographer again. Not a studio hack, but an artist. He'd print the best one and give it to Joe. Or maybe print two copies so he could put one on his own wall. He thought of exhibitions for the first time since Laos. These shots were worth it. What would complement them? What would make them stronger?

That night, he dreamt of Joe.

Joe, grabbing him, saying 'don't get too close', but kissing him all the same, mouth as hungry as the waves. Alex woke as he came, hand on his own dick, pleasure singing through him even as Joe faded away from his embrace. He hadn't had a wet dream in years. Didn't think he *could*, any more. He should just enjoy that it had happened. But somehow, he felt lonelier than ever.

***

Alex caught Joe looking at him sometimes, with a steady, considering gaze that turned into a smile and a blush if Alex noticed him doing it. In any other guy, he'd have thought it a giveaway, but while Joe would listen to his stories or ideas about photography with rapt attention, he never quite tipped the scales into flirtation. Despite the way he bared his soul in his comics, there was something reserved about Joe in person. Even his social media was all about his art, alongside an occasional photo of Blue. As a profile picture, Joe used a drawing of himself, a big-eyed, anxious-looking caricature that was both very like and very unlike the real Joe.

And Joe always refused to be photographed, which made Alex's heart ache in a very particular way. After a couple of hours of talking and sketching, Joe would say, "I'd better go now," and could never be persuaded to stay. He'd smile and shake his head, not breaking step as he slipped out the front door.

Alex still wondered sometimes about the comics in which 'Joe' was in love with the mermaid, and the comics with the Prince Frog. He'd watched Joe kick Sean out of his life, and it was clear that Sean had been some sort of sexual partner. But Joe had told him that he'd gone out with Blessing—yes, that really was her name—for several years after leaving the commune where they'd both grown up. It hadn't worked out. She'd gone back to commune life, somewhere up north. Joe had stayed away, though he seemed to bear the commune people no ill will. So, had Sean been a one-off? If he'd been an experiment, he'd evidently been a pretty unpleasant one.

Of course, Alex could have asked Joe outright where his preferences lay, but to ask would be to state a sexual interest, and he wasn't ready to put everything on the line like that. He and Joe were neighbours; if Alex made an unwanted pass, they would both have to live with it. Alex was avoiding enough; he didn't want to have to avoid Joe as well. For now, it was enough to go fishing with Joe, or find him sketching on the beach, or to have him lighting up the occasional evening with his gentle humour and fierce anti-commercialism.

One morning, Alex woke early and couldn't go back to sleep. He listened to the birds twittering in the hedge outside his window, and thought of Laos. Of the water buffalo wallowing in potholes on the road, of women with yellow rice powder on their faces, and the taste of indifferent noodles at a roadside stand. He couldn't help but think of Aoife, drinking Laotian beer out of the bottle, the sleeves of her white shirt rolled up, discussing the next day's schedule. In that moment, with the birds sounding like little bells in the hedge, he was able to contemplate what had happened to her, and to Khamane, and what had nearly happened to him, and then take his thoughts away, in a way he'd never been able to before.

All the same, it seemed a bad idea to go on lying there with nothing to distract him. The severed foot and the taste of blood and the fear were at bay this morning, but they were still there. Probably, they would never go away. He got up, and seeing the dawn light at the edges of the curtains, thought he'd go down to the beach and maybe bump into Joe, who often went fishing early. He opened the front door and Joe was sitting on the step, as if he'd been waiting.

"Hi," Alex said, warmth bursting inside his chest.

"Hi." Joe stood up.

There was something in his tone of voice that made Alex say, "You okay?"

"Well, actually, I just wanted to see you."

"Yeah?" Another wave of warm honey. *Calm down; he probably wants to borrow a piece of string or take some bacon rind for bait.*

Joe stretched, winced. "Gosh, it was cold sitting there. Can I come in?"

"Breakfast?"

Alex didn't wait for an answer. Joe was always hungry. Alex had put on the kettle and got out the pan to scramble eggs when he realised Joe hadn't sat down at the kitchen table, as he usually did, but was standing next to it, arms wrapped around himself, rubbing his left shoulder.

"What's up?" Alex said.

Joe sighed. "I had a bad night. That's all. I don't sleep so well, sometimes. My shoulder aches. You know, from the crash."

They were about two feet apart. It felt right to close the distance between them, to put a hand on Joe's upper arm. "Sucks, eh?"

Joe nodded and took a step forward, letting Alex hold him. Joe's shaggy, glossy hair was like silk against Alex's cheek. Joe smelled of wood smoke and wool, and the cold was still coming off him. Alex's mouth was near Joe's jawline. He thought he could feel Joe's heart pounding, but probably it was his own. If Joe had turned his head a fraction to the left, if he had stayed one second longer, Alex would have kissed him.

But Joe moved away. "It's all right telling you. You get it."

"Yeah. I do." Behind Alex, the kettle clicked off. Joe was sitting down, getting out his sketchbook.

"Want to talk about it?" Alex said.

"Nah, just wanted to see you," Joe said to the sketchbook. He was drawing a salt shaker with its arms around a surprised-looking bottle of wine. A couple of supercilious wine glasses were watching, eyebrows raised. "A friend's getting me some weed today. That usually helps."

"That's good."

Joe bent over his drawing. "It's illegal. You don't think it's wrong?"

"I think you're hardly a menace to society. I'd probably do the same if I were you."

They had breakfast and Joe went home. Alex had a job that day, a shoot for an insurance company's corporate brochures. But the sensation of Joe in his arms would not leave him. He photographed smiling families and senior citizens in brightly coloured clothes and thought of Joe.

Of course, Joe could come for comfort and breakfast after a bad night. It was a good thing Alex hadn't kissed him. Only an asshole kissed a friend who needed a hug.

But was Joe using him? Leading him on? Joe never let things get too far. So, he'd always have somewhere warm to go, with food laid on, while Alex got more and more smitten. And in summer, Joe would probably turn up with a new girlfriend, or a new boyfriend, and Alex would wish they'd never met.

Except, it wasn't like that. Joe wasn't like that. And if Joe did turn up with a girlfriend or boyfriend, what would it matter? Because Alex was too old for him anyway. Joe still got pimples sometimes. Alex had started finding ear hairs like copper wire, and his stubble grew in more grey than brown these days. Joe was twenty-six. Nearly two decades younger. And anyway, Alex wasn't ready for a relationship.

Ah, but the feel of him in my arms, wood smoke in his hair, my knees weak, and that sweet ache in my chest because I want him so much.

Chapter Five

A couple of weeks later, Alex took a call from Chris, an old friend from London. Chris and his partner Miguel were in Sydney. Coming to New Zealand for a week. Could they stay a couple of nights? The trip had been planned for the last year. Finally, it was happening. Chris proposed going out on Friday night—dinner, the theatre—then back to Alex's.

"Sure," Alex said, "I'll make bookings."

At the studio, he started to buy tickets for a play at the theatre down on the Wellington waterfront, something about love in the age of dating apps. Three tickets. But why not four? Why not invite Joe? Alex had told Joe he had friends coming to stay sometime soon. Joe had been happy for him. So, Alex reserved four tickets, and four for dinner at Logan Brown, one of the fancier restaurants in Wellington.

That evening, he almost overshot Joe's driveway and had to brake hard to make the turn. He'd decided it would be better to invite Joe in person than to trust to patchy mobile reception, but his stomach was churning and his hands were slick on the wheel.

Always, in the past, Alex had slept with guys first, and sometimes fallen in love afterwards. To be in love with someone who wasn't already a lover felt ridiculous, immature, like lusting after someone in high school. It was the traditional way straight people did it: get to know the person, fall in love, have sex. Did it always feel this excruciating? How on earth had he allowed it to happen? Normally, he managed his love life better than this. Though of course, since Laos, his love life had either been non-existent or a disaster.

Blue strolled over, reaching his head over the fence for a pat as Alex got out of the car.

The problem was, Joe wasn't just another potential lover. Even the phrase 'love life' felt reductive when he thought of Joe. Because being with Joe wasn't some compartmentalised thing that Alex did in his spare time. It was everything.

Being with Joe made him feel braver, kinder, more capable. And he *admired* Joe. Admired his dedication to comics and his determination not to be swayed by fashion or money or what was cool. It wasn't that Joe was oblivious. He knew very well that his snowflake sweater was ugly, so he made it into a joke, but—and this seemed crucial—he wore it anyway. Joe knew his car was shitty and his hair unkempt, but he chose not to care so he could put his energy into the things that really mattered to him. Alex had met plenty of desperately hip people in London and New York who claimed never to worry about what people thought of them. But it was Joe, for all his shyness, who was the closest thing to free that Alex had ever seen.

He took a deep breath and knocked on the door.

Joe answered it. "Want to come in?"

There was a faint smell of marijuana coming from him. Perhaps his shoulder had been aching. But he didn't look stoned. He never smoked much, or drank much, because his finances were too precarious.

"Bella should be here in a minute," Joe added. He grinned, gorgeous as a Helmut Newton celebrity. "Guess what? I think she's got a girlfriend. She's been sending the most cryptic messages and her Instagram's gone all sexy and noir."

"Really? Well, good for her. No, I won't come in. I wanted to ask you…remember I told you about Chris and Miguel? They're arriving next Friday, and we're going out to dinner and to that new play down at Circa Theatre. Would you like to come? I'd love it if you joined us."

Joe's eyes widened in alarm. Then he frowned. "You don't want me along. You'll be with your friends."

"Of course, I want you along. I'm inviting you. My treat, obviously."

"Oh no, really. I couldn't."

"I hope it's not about me paying, because you've already given me a fortune in fresh fish if we're worrying about things like that. Won't you come?"

"It's not that."

"No? Good. So, what do you say? You needn't be shy. These are my friends. It's like me meeting Rawiri or Bella."

But Joe had gone bright red and mulish and was glaring at the threadbare doormat. "Sorry, I…I can't. I've got to get some work done."

The butterflies that had buoyed Alex up all day flitted away. But it sounded so much like an excuse that he said, "Couldn't you do the work another day? They're only here for a couple of nights. I'd like you to meet them. Chris was my first friend in London, like you're my first friend here."

Chris had been his lover too, for a while, but he wasn't going to mention that.

"No, sorry, but I…I mean, maybe another night."

"Well, never mind." Alex couldn't hide the disappointment in his voice. "See you around."

He got back in his car feeling like an utter fool. It was nothing like the sting of rejection from a stranger in a bar. It hurt to the bone, because the lines of the friendship had been defined. Sure, Joe might be shy of meeting new people, but he knew Alex well enough by now to be honest about that. This refusal meant something more. Hanging out at Alex's place was clearly one thing, going out with Alex on something resembling a real date was another. Joe was twenty-six and a handsome artist. Even if he was shy, he could find the balls to make a move on Alex if he wanted. But Joe didn't want to. So, he hadn't.

Perhaps Joe didn't want an aging teetotaller with mental problems and an empty social calendar. Perhaps he wanted a lover he could go out and have fun with. *Quelle sur-fucking-prise.*

It was true dark when Alex got home, but he went for a run anyway. Made dinner. Ate half of it. Spent hours tinkering with the shots for the insurance company, checked his email, sent invoices. If he'd had any scotch in the house he'd have drunk it. He kept thinking of Joe, saying no, not once, but several times. Since when had Alex become the kind of guy who wouldn't take no for an answer? It was pathetic. *He* was pathetic. Eventually he took a sleeping pill, his first since moving to Kahawai Bay, and passed out.

He spent Friday half-waiting for a piece of white paper to appear under the door bearing a droll little sketch expressing that Joe would like to go to the theatre after all. But no such thing eventuated. As the sun began to set, Alex walked into Makara Beach to get phone reception and received a series of texts from Miguel; they were driving down from Rotorua, having seen bubbling mud. They had seen Mt. Ruapehu and the Desert Road. They were sharing their hire car with an English back-packer they'd met in Rotorua.

'*He thinks ur hot. Wanna meet him?*' Miguel sent a photo of a blue-eyed blond, about thirty-five, sun-tanned and smiling, one eyebrow crooked as a geyser exploded behind him.

They had room at the table, a spare ticket for the theatre that Joe didn't want. Joe wasn't interested. Why not meet this guy?

* * *

Seeing Chris and Miguel again was better than good. Alex had known Chris for fifteen years, first as lovers and then as friends. When they'd met, Chris had been a personal trainer with bleached blond hair and the best body in the club. Now, he was an Inspector for the Met and looked like a cop, even out of uniform. He and Miguel had been together for twelve years. Miguel, a social worker, had the same dark eyes as Joe, but he was twice Joe's size, with olive skin and short-cropped hair.

There was something reassuring about being with people who'd known him before Laos, who knew he didn't normally make brides cry on their wedding day, who knew that once upon a time he used to drink and dance and have fun and follow current events like any well-informed adult.

'The guy who thinks you're hot' was called William. He was a lawyer taking a year off to see the world. Despite being a back-packer, he wore an expensive blue cashmere sweater that hugged his pecs, and he clearly thought he was the smartest person in the room. Alex was inclined to hate him immediately —for his sharp, unforgiving eyes, his over-confident handshake and the contemptuous edge in his voice when the waitress brought him the wrong drink.

Joe would have smiled and said it didn't matter. Joe had sympathy for the human condition; he forgave people for not being perfect. Then Alex realised he was probably hating William for not being Joe. At one time, he wouldn't have minded William's cutting sense of humour, would have liked his snarky, sarcastic edge. He made an effort to smile at some of William's kinder jokes.

As the evening wore on, it became clear that William was angling to come home with them—with *him*. Alex felt he'd rather invite in one of the huge spiky bugs that lived in the woodshed, but gradually, his revulsion morphed into something more ambivalent. Later still, it became almost fatalistic. William wanted it, and what William wanted, William got. And it would be nice not to sleep alone for once. It would be nice to have sex that wasn't solo, or part of a dream, and to feel someone's arms around him. He could always pretend it was someone sweeter, someone he actually liked.

When the time came to leave, William said, "Shall I join you out in the sticks?"

Alex shrugged. "It's not flash." A surge of self-preservation made him add, "But there's a spare couch if you don't mind that."

At least that way he had an out, if William became unbearable.

William smiled under his lashes, as if to say, *we all know that's not going to happen* and said aloud, "All right. We'll see, shall we?"

They were walking along the waterfront, the black harbour reflecting the lights of Wellington, when Alex's phone rang. He pulled it out, stomach clenching when he saw the caller ID: Joe Taylor.

"Hi."

"Alex, I'm sorry to call, but I need a favour. If you don't mind. I'm sorry."

Hearing Joe's voice, after an evening spent with William, was a reminder of a kinder, gentler world. It hurt.

"What's up?" Alex said.

"The thing is, my car won't start, and I—"

Joe sounded strained, like he was expecting Alex to yell at him.

"Need a ride?" Alex said. *Don't you get that I'd do anything for you?* "Sure. Are you in town? I'm with Chris and Miguel, and, ah, a friend of theirs. We're heading home. We're nearly at the car. It's good timing."

"I'm really sorry, Alex, but I've no money, and I've tried everyone else. I can't ask Juleke, and Ra's got the kids, and everyone else has been drinking because it's Friday night. But you haven't, have you?"

"No," Alex said.

He felt a spurt of irritation that Joe had rung him last and only out of desperation. But then, Joe had been avoiding him since refusing to come out tonight. So, why else would he ring? Joe was scrupulously careful about not drinking and driving, or getting in a car with anyone who'd been drinking or taking drugs.

"The thing is, I'm in Porirua East." Joe's voice wobbled.

"What are you doing there? Isn't that pretty dodgy?"

Silence. He could hear Joe breathing.

"All right?" Chris said. He had a cop's nose for trouble.

"Promise you won't be angry?" Joe said.

"Probably. Try me," Alex said. They'd reached the dark car park. Alex unlocked his car so the others could get in. Miguel and William got in the back, Chris in the passenger seat.

"I was buying weed," Joe said.

"Oh, Joe. Out there?"

"I usually get it off someone else. But he's away, and his flatmate said to come here, and now my car won't start and it's kind of scary. I'd walk, but it's too far. And